THE ROOSTER'S GIFT

BY PAM CONRAD

PICTURES BY ERIC BEDDOWS

A LAURA GERINGER BOOK
An Imprint of HarperCollins Publishers

Library of Congress Cataloging-in-Publication Data
Conrad, Pam.
    The rooster's gift / by Pam Conrad ; pictures by Eric Beddows.
        p.   cm.
    "A Laura Geringer book."
    Summary : Young Rooster thinks his Gift is making the sun rise, until one morning when the sun rises with-
out him.
    ISBN 0-06-023603-5. — ISBN 0-06-023604-3 (lib. bdg.)
    [1. Roosters—Fiction.   2. Chickens—Fiction.   3. Pride and vanity—Fiction.]   I. Beddows, Eric, date ill.
II. Title.
PZ7.C76476Ro   1996   93-14490
[E]—dc20   CIP
                                                                                                      AC

Typography by Christine Kettner
1   2   3   4   5   6   7   8   9   10
❖
First Edition

For Elliott
—E.B.

ONCE UP ON A HILL, in a brand-new chicken coop, there were ten tiny chicks who had just broken out of their eggs, dried off, fluffed themselves up and looked around.

An old farmer and his wife looked down on them and the chicks heard the woman say, "Sure hope one of them's a rooster."

Then the old couple left the chicks to wonder.

"Where are we?" wondered one chick.

"What's a rooster?" asked another.

"Hope I'm a rooster," said still another.

And they all spoke with little peeps, squeaks and cheeps.

"I think I'm a rooster," said one little chick, and they all turned to look at him.

"What makes you think so?" they asked.

"Just a feeling," he said.

And they looked at him strangely, because instead of speaking in peeps and squeaks and cheeps, this particular chick spoke in glickles and gorks and flonks. Something was definitely different about this one.

The old farmer's wife brought them food every morning. Corn, grain and seeds. She scattered them on the dirt and watched the chicks carefully. And every day they grew a little more. Soon they changed from fluffy little chicks to bigger chicks to hens. And instead of speaking with peeps and squeaks and cheeps, they started speaking with bok-boks and cackles.

Except for one. The different one. When he spoke it was beginning to sound like "Ca-tockle, ca-tockle, flonk."

"That's our rooster, all right," the old woman said one day, pointing him out to the old farmer.

The Young Rooster thrust out his chest and swelled with pride.

"Sure hope he's got the Gift," the old woman said, and she went away.

"What'd she say?" bok-bokked one hen.

"What's the Gift?" cackled another.

"Sure wish I had the Gift," cheeped still another.

"I believe I do have the Gift," said the Young Rooster, and they all circled around him.

"What makes you think so?" they asked.

"Just a feeling," he said.

Then one night, very late, very, *very* late, past late to something
else, the Young Rooster awoke in the dark coop. All his sisters were
sleeping. He closed his eyes and tried to sleep again, but something
would not let him.

It's the Gift, he thought. Very carefully he stood and tried to
leave the coop without making any noise. But all the hens heard him
and sleepily followed their brother out into the blackness that covered
the hill.

"What's he doing?" asked one.

"He's acting so strange," said another.

"Maybe it's the Gift," whispered yet another.

The Young Rooster took two hops and found himself standing atop the chicken coop with all his sisters standing below. He couldn't help himself. Something pushed him up there.

A quiet hush fell over the chickens, over the hill, over the sky. Young Rooster tightened his feet on the rim of the coop, closed his eyes, stretched his body far, far, high and high into the night and then—

"Cot Cot Cot Cot Ca-toodle tooooooo!"

The chickens stared at him.

"Get down from there," scolded one.

"My, my," worried another.

Then again, louder and wilder—

"Cot Cot Cot Cot Ca-toodle TOOOOOO!" Young Rooster was glorious. He felt lifted up, charged, holy.

He ignored the chickens scolding him, but then he heard one gasp, "Look! Look!"

Young Rooster was facing east. He opened his eyes. A streak of orange shot across the horizon. Yellows pirouetted into the clouds. Slowly, slowly but so surely, the sky ran from black, to indigo, to blue.

"Look what you've done, Rooster! Look what you've done!"

"Look what I've done," Rooster repeated, and he was weak with joy. "It's the Gift," he told them. "I make the day. That's my Gift."

The truly glorious part of the Gift was that it didn't happen just that once. It happened every single morning. Young Rooster would wake in the night for no reason, strut out into the brisk air, hop up onto the roof of the coop and give out a mighty "Cot Cot Cot Cot Ca-toodle too!" and the day would begin. He was amazing.

Now it wasn't that the hens got used to it or anything, but after a week or so they didn't follow him out into the darkness to watch anymore. They'd sit in their feathers and straw with their eyes open the slightest bit, and they'd listen to his strong feet skip across the roof of the chicken coop.

"Cot Cot Cot Cot Ca-toodle tooooooo!" they'd hear him cry. And ever so slowly they'd watch as the inside of the chicken coop would begin to glow and grow bright. They were proud of their Young Rooster, but they didn't need to watch anymore.

Except for one of them, that is. The smallest.

She would wake as soon as he did and follow him out of the coop into the darkness. She would stand there on the grass and watch as he'd bound up onto the roof, stretch himself high and high against the stars and cry his call across the valley. Then the smallest hen would face the east and smile as the colors appeared, and the sun would answer. Even on rainy mornings she would stand there, the drops glistening on her soft feathers, and watch as the darkness would turn to mist and the pale tender day would begin.

Smallest Hen would wait until the sun was well up in the sky, and then she'd say to Young Rooster, "Thank you, Rooster."

In the beginning he'd grin and hop down from his perch to be by her. And they'd talk about his Gift. But eventually, after smiling slightly, he would be on his way. Soon he would only nod. Then barely nod. And finally he didn't even hear her. Rooster was growing very proud of this Gift. Very, very proud.

Day after day, Young Rooster began the day, and days turned into seasons and seasons into years. The hens laid eggs, and what the old farmer's wife didn't take away in her basket became tiny chicks. Rooster had stopped sleeping in the crowded coop long ago, but still Smallest Hen continued to wake up in time to watch him make the day.

One night Smallest Hen woke up
and ruffled her feathers. Her sisters
and their chicks snored all around her.
She tiptoed over the straw and feathers,
out the door to the grass. For the first
morning that Smallest Hen could
remember, Rooster was nowhere in
sight, so Smallest Hen snuggled down
onto the grass and waited.

No Rooster.
No Rooster.
Still no Rooster.

Smallest Hen looked over the hills. It was dark. She couldn't see a thing. Where was Rooster? She squinted into the woods. No Rooster. She stood and began walking in chicken circles. What if something had happened to him? Who would start the day?

She peered off into the woods again. They were dark against a lightening sky. He wasn't coming from the woods. She looked again over the hills that were growing brighter. He wasn't coming over the hills. She looked into the sky as two swallows crisscrossed above her. She looked east at the sun that was coming up in the valley. "Well, I'll be plucked," she whispered. "The sun came up anyway."

Rooster came panting up behind her. His feathers were wild. His wings were flapping. His tail was awry. "What's going on?" he shouted. "How could you go on without me?"

Smallest Hen shrugged. "It just happened," she said. "I was standing here waiting for you. I didn't do a thing, and before I knew it, the hills lightened, the valley grew bright and the sun came up."

"Without me," he whispered. "Without me."

Smallest Hen nodded. "Without you," she agreed.

Rooster turned and walked away from her toward the valley.

She called after him, "But it's much better *with* you."

But Rooster didn't hear her. He was looking at the sun that no longer looked like his.

The next day Smallest Hen awoke as usual and went outside.
Rooster was there in the darkness, standing on the roof of the coop.
He didn't make a sound. He was very still. And she watched him.
Gradually the sky lightened, the valley came to life and the sun lifted
in the east. "I don't believe it," Rooster muttered, and he went away.

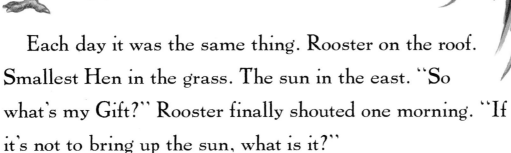

Each day it was the same thing. Rooster on the roof.
Smallest Hen in the grass. The sun in the east. "So
what's my Gift?" Rooster finally shouted one morning. "If
it's not to bring up the sun, what is it?"

"Maybe the Gift is that you know when the sun is about to
come up," she suggested.

Rooster stared at her. "That makes no sense whatsoever. What good
is that? Even *you* know when the sun is about to come up."

Smallest Hen fluffed and blushed, for she knew this was true. "But
it's you who call to the sun," she told him.

"Ridiculous," he said. "Anyone could do it. Even you."

The next morning he tried to show her. In the darkness he pushed her up onto the roof. He eased her along the edge out to the peak. "Hold on here," he said, showing her how to wrap her toes around the edge. "Now stretch up."

She grew round and fat.

"Stretch up!" he shouted.

"I am!"

"No you're not. You're getting round and fat."

"It's the best I can do," she said.

Rooster shook his head. "All right now. Wait awhile and when it feels right, yell, 'Cot Cot Cot Cot Ca-toodle too.'"

She looked at him doubtfully. She was afraid to be this high up on the roof. She wrapped her toes around the edge. She hunkered down into her round fat body, waited, waited, and then when the moment felt right, when the sun felt like a big fat egg about to emerge from the darkness, she cried, "Bok-bok ca-bok ca-bok ca-bok!"

Rooster was aghast. "What was that?" he said.

Smallest Hen was embarrassed. Terribly embarrassed. "Well, you needn't make fun." She fell to the ground in a whirl of feathers.

Rooster hopped down after her. "I'm not making fun."

"It was the best I could do," she huffed.

"Yes," he said. "I believe you, and I'm beginning to understand."

"About the Gift?" she asked.

He nodded. "I know when the sun is about to rise," he told her. "And so do you, Smallest Hen."

"Yes, somehow I know when it's coming," she admitted.

"But you can't announce it quite the same," he said.

Smallest Hen snorted. "That's apparent."

He thought for a while and then smiled at her. "I do it quite well, don't I?"

"You do it very well, Rooster. I always loved the way you did it."

"I guess that's the Gift," he said quietly. "Not quite like pulling the sun out of the night, but a Gift nonetheless, wouldn't you say?"

"I'd say so," Smallest Hen answered.

That night, very late, very, *very* late, past late
to something else, Old Rooster took two hops and
stood atop the chicken coop. Blackness covered
the hill and a quiet hush slept in the hollows of the
valley. Old Rooster held very still, tightened his
feet over the rim of the coop, closed his eyes,
stretched his body far, far, high and high into the
night and then—

"Cot Cot Cot Cot Ca-toodle tooooooo!"

And then together Old Rooster and Smallest Hen watched as a streak
of pink shot across the hills into the valley, and yellows bathed the trees,
and blues melted across the sky and the sun rose like the most glorious
egg in the world.

"Well done, Rooster," bok-bokked Smallest Hen. "Well done."